This book
belongs to:

Rocket's Very
Fine Day

To Grampa Fred and Nancy,
who make a cloudy day sunny!

Copyright © 2019 by Tad Hills

All rights reserved. Published in the United States by Schwartz & Wade Books, an imprint of Random House Children's Books, a division of Penguin Random House LLC, New York.

Schwartz & Wade Books and the colophon are trademarks of Penguin Random House LLC.

Visit us on the Web! rhcbooks.com

Educators and librarians, for a variety of teaching tools, visit us at RHTeachersLibrarians.com

Library of Congress Cataloging-in-Publication Data
Name: Hills, Tad, author, illustrator.
Title: Rocket's very fine day / Tad Hills.
Description: First edition. | New York: Schwartz & Wade Books, [2019] | Summary: Rocket and his friend Bella plan to spend the day outside, but their perfect day is nearly ruined by the rain.
Identifiers: LCCN 2018055453
ISBN 978-0-525-64493-4 (hardback) | ISBN 978-0-525-64495-8 (hardcover library binding)
ISBN 978-0-525-64496-5 (ebook) | ISBN 978-0-525-64494-1 (paperback)
Subjects: | CYAC: Rain and rainfall—Fiction. | Play—Fiction. | Dogs—Fiction. | Squirrels—Fiction. | BISAC: JUVENILE FICTION / Animals / Dogs. | JUVENILE FICTION / Social Issues / Friendship. | JUVENILE FICTION / Imagination & Play.
Classification: LCC PZ7.H563737 Rq 2019 | DDC [E]—dc23

The text of this book is set in 24-point Century.
The illustrations were rendered in colored pencils and acrylic paint.

MANUFACTURED IN CHINA

10 9 8 7 6 5 4 3 2 1

Rocket's Very Fine Day

Tad Hills

schwartz & wade books · new york

"We are lucky
it is a sunny day,"
says Bella.

Rocket counts only
one cloud in the sky.

Rocket and Bella
play in the meadow
all morning.

They play hide-and-seek
in the tall grass.

Bella chases Rocket.

Rocket chases Bella.

They walk across logs.

They play fetch
until they are tired.

They rest and
count the clouds.

But now there are
too many clouds
to count.

It is not sunny
anymore.

Bella feels a raindrop.

Rocket feels
a raindrop, too.

Soon it is raining hard.

"Oh no!" cries Bella.
"I do not like
the rain."

Rocket and Bella
sit under a tree
to stay dry.

They watch the rain
come down.

"I do not like the rain," says Bella. "But I do like . . ."

"PUDDLES!"

Rocket and Bella splash
in big puddles.

They splash
in small puddles.

They splash
in deep puddles.

They splash in
muddy puddles.

The rain stops
and the sun
comes out.

They splash

some more!

When the sun sets,
they stop splashing
and they rest.

"We are lucky
it was a rainy day,"
says Bella.
"Yes, lucky indeed,"
Rocket agrees.